TO MADDY,

HELLO FROM STANLEY & NORMAN !

StaNlEy & NoRMaN
bad boy bassEt bRothERs

Written by Frank Monahan
Illustrated by Deborah FitzGerald

Credits
Written and Produced by Frank Monahan
Illustrated by Deborah FitzGerald
Edited by Karen R. Monahan
Graphic Design by Meredith Hancock

© 2008 Rocket Science Productions
ISBN-13: 978-0-9821823-0-7
ISBN-10: 0-9821823-0-9

Library of Congress Control Number: 2008940002

Stanley and Norman are Basset Hound Brothers.

NORMAN   STANLEY

7

They live in a nice house...

... with the Mama, the Daddy, the Sister, and the Brother.

They also have a big yard to run and play in all day.

They love to jump
and play
in their big backyard.

There's a lot to explore.

One day in the yard, Stanley heard a funny sound.

It was a meowing sound, and it came from the next yard.

"Let's go play with the cats, Norman," said Stanley.

"We can't," said Norman.
"They're on the other side of the fence."

"But it would be fun
to go over there," said Stanley.
"It could be an adventure."

"The Mama said we might get lost, or hurt,"
said Norman. "We should stay here."

17

"I want to go play with the cats, and that's what I'm going to do," Stanley said, and he began digging under the fence.

Soon they were running in the next yard, but this yard had no fence on the other side like their yard, and they couldn't see the cats anywhere.

They sniffed and sniffed the ground
with their hound dog noses,
trying to find where the cats went.

Soon they were far down the street
and couldn't find the cats anywhere.

"Stanley, the cats must have gone home, but now I can't see our house."

"I think we're lost."

"I think it's this way, Norman," said Stanley.
"No, it isn't, Stanley," replied Norman.

"Oh no, Stanley, we are lost. We can't find home."
Norman was getting worried.

Just then, they heard a sound they knew.
It was the clinking sound of their walking leashes.
They also heard a voice they knew right away.

Coming down the street calling them loudly was the Daddy.
Norman...Stanley," cried out the Daddy.
"Where are you, Boys?"

Just then, the
Daddy saw Stanley
& Norman in
another yard.

"Boys, you aren't supposed to be out of your yard," said the Daddy.
"You could get lost or hurt."
"Let's go home and play in your yard where it's safe."

Stanley & Norman walked home
quietly with the Daddy.

25

They were finally back in their own yard where the Daddy
got busy fixing the hole that Stanley & Norman made to get out.

"No more adventures for today," said the Mama. "And no more going out of the yard without the Mama or the Daddy."

"Let's get a nice, cool drink of water...

...and then take a little nap, safe and snug, in our own yard."